GIORGIO SALATI

CHRISTIAN CORNIA

BRINA the CAT

The Gang of the Feline Sun

PAPERCUTZ
New York

THE SMURFS #21

THE ONLY LIVING GIRL #1

BARBIE #1

THE SISTERS #1

CAT & CAT #1

GERONIMO STILTON #17

THEA STILTON #6

FUZZY BASEBALL

DINOSAUR EXPLORERS #1

SCARLETT

ANNE OF GREEN BAGELS #1

DRACULA MARRIES FRANKENSTEIN!

THE RED SHOES

THE LITTLE MERMAID

GERONIMO STILTON REPORTER #1

HOTEL TRANSYLVANIA #1

THE LOUD HOUSE #1

MANOSAURS #1

THE ONLY LIVING BOY #5

GUMBY #1

MORE GREAT GRAPHIC NOVEL SERIES AVAILABLE FROM

PAPERCUTZ™

papercutz.com

All available where ebooks are sold.

Foreword by Frédéric Brrémaud and Federico Bertolucci

To Daisy, Susy and Tea: the flowers of my garden.

−Giorgio

To Erika for her continued support, to Tommy,
And to Otto, Leo, Samantha, and Nicole for their "hairy" company.

−Christian

*Special thanks to Teresa Radice & Stefano Turconi, Marie Garot,
the editorial team at Topolino, Ken Anderson, and Milt Kahl.*

#1 "The Gang of the Feline Sun"

©2020 TUNUÉ (Tunué s.r.l) - Giorgio Salati and Christian Cornia
Originally published in Italy as *Brina e la Banda del Sole Felino* by
TUNUÉ (Tunué s.r.l.) in 2017. All rights reserved. www.tunue.com
All other editorial material ©2020 by Papercutz.
www.papercutz.com

GIORGIO SALATI — Script
CHRISTIAN CORNIA — Art, Color, and Cover
ERIKA TURBATI — Color Assistance
MASSIMILIANO CLEMENTE — Original Editor
ALESSANDRO AURELI — Lettering and Layout
OLIVIA ROSE DONI — Translation
Foreword by FRÉDÉRIC BRRÉMAUD and FEDERICO BERTOLUCCI
Special Thanks to CECILIA RANERI

JEFF WHITMAN — Editor, Production
IZZY BOYCE-BLANCHARD — Editorial Intern
JIM SALICRUP
Editor-in-Chief

Papercutz books may be purchased for business or promotional use.
For information on bulk purchases please contact
Macmillan Corporate and Premium Sales Department at
(800) 221-795 x5442.

Hardcover ISBN: 978-1-5458-0425-4
Paperback ISBN: 978-1-5458-0426-1

Printed in China
January 2020

Distributed by Macmillan
First Papercutz Printing

6

7

And the following morning, the scent of herbs and prey instills a new energy in Brina.

SHOULD WE LET HER OUT AGAIN?

WHY NOT? AND FOR BREAKFAST WE CAN HAVE THAT FANTASTIC RYE BREAD THEY MAKE HERE.

WOOF! WOOF! WOOF!

WOOF!

AND SO... HERE IS THE HALF-CAT.

THE CAGED ONE WHO LIVES WITH HUMANS.

?

OH... YOU COWARD!

WOOF! ...

11

GRR...

WOOF!

WOOF!

HUH, LOOK WHO'S BACK. DON'T TELL ME YOU FREED YOURSELF FROM YOUR PRISON?

EXACTLY.

24

Sam fears that if Brina reaches the main road, she could be hit by a car.

BRINA?

But she's always been afraid of cars, she would never go near them.

Unless her desire for adventure has become too strong.

8.07

The air is clear and crisp.
The stars are like drops in a teary sky.

It would be a perfect night, if the young couple's hearts weren't beating softly, like bare feet on the thin ice of hope.

It would be wonderful to wake up and find the cat rolled up on his lap...

...like before. A very recent past for humans, but so long ago for a feline.

For the moment, there is only a near silence, never absolute, for that is the sound of Nature. Every creature distinctly recognizable. Except one.

Except Brina.

A MOUSE!

I GUESS YOU HAVEN'T SEEN MANY, HOLED UP IN AN APARTMENT.

SQUEAK!

WHAT JOY! I HAVEN'T FELT LIKE THIS SINCE...

...SINCE I WAS IN THE COUNTRY. THEN... THEN I WAS FREE.

GOT IT!

MOM! IT GOT AWAY!

DON'T WORRY, BRINA, THE NEXT ONE WILL BE YOURS.

The morning sun peers over the mountains like a child from under his bed covers.

And the cat hasn't come back.

Brina's mind is like a clear blue sky.

She and her friends challenge each other to see who can climb the fastest up the huge gnarly trees that stand guard in the forest.

In the meantime, Sam and Margret put up the fliers in the village.

They might have to pay a fine, but they don't really care.

Their concern for Brina pushes them to act quickly. Sam wants to get everything finished as soon as possible.

While Margret's mind is fighting back her emotions. Like a pond whose surface is constantly disturbed.

The couple chases passersby.

They politely listen to stories that have nothing to do with their search and which they don't really want to waste time on.

YOU KNOW, UP UNTIL LAST MONTH WE HAD A LOVELY LITTLE BLACK CAT...

Meanwhile, Brina is busy chasing all kinds of prey.

Those who manage to escape her go tell their friends what happened to them.

A quick break, drinking from the stream like true wild animals.

And bingo! The first catch as a liberated cat. Time for a snack, finally.

Time for a snack for Sam too: his stomach is rumbling, aided by stress. Margret doesn't understand: how can he possibly eat right now?

Why spend money, when there are fountains and wild strawberries galore? Sam can't understand: how can she think about money right now?

"We shouldn't have let her out."

"She's a city cat, she's not used to being out."

Sam tries to console her: Brina might be a city cat, but she was born in the country. She has her wild instincts, she'll manage just fine.

Instinct.

Instinct tells Sam to check under the cars.

His heart skips a beat.

But it's not her. She just looks like her.

"It must be the cat of the lady from the copy shop," says Sam.

"This is what our Brina looks like," they say, pointing at the flyer. "We mustn't forget her.

BRINA
LOST
2-YEAR-OLD TABBY.
IF YOU FIND HER,
PLEASE CALL US
AT THIS NUMBER:
555-555-9706

"Ever."

BRINA...

IS... IS IT HER?

IT'S JUST... A PLASTIC BAG.

BRINA!

BRINA?

Brina doesn't know who or what to believe.

Trust humans again? How could she, if she can't even trust her fellow cats?

Brina is hungry, and cold, and alone. But going back home would be a defeat. Wouldn't it?

Brina's mind is no longer a clear blue sky. The stars are hiding.

The only lights that shine in her memories are her mother's eyes.

Brina was just a little over two months old when Sam and Margret turned up at the farm.

HERE ARE THE KITTENS. WE ALREADY HAVE THREE CATS AND THE COWS TOO, SO WE HAVE TO GIVE THEM AWAY.

64

CHOOSE THE ONE YOU PREFER. ALL OF THEM, IF YOU LIKE.

WE CAN'T TAKE MORE THAN ONE. WE LIVE IN AN APARTMENT, IN THE CITY.

THE ONE WITH THE COLORED SPOTS, THE FADED ONE...

IT'S A GIRL, RIGHT?

YES, IT'S A GIRL.

WHAT IS SHE DOING? SHE'S LICKING THE WALL?!

SHE'S SO FUNNY.

That night the sky is a slippery surface that the clouds slide across, revealing the pale moonlight.

The stars are shining again in Brina's eyes. Now she feels like a real cat.

She finally understands what whiskers are for.

The incredible sense of smell.

It's all to get back to those we love.

Those sharp eyes that can see in the dark.

That keen instinct.

And after the mountain, it is the turn of the forest, the stream, the clouds, and the sun to all say goodbye.

A sun that looks over the peaks. A star that warms your steps, wherever they may take you. A new star that bounces inside you like the beat of a rattle, and makes you dance with its crystalline notes.

A free and welcoming sun.

A feline sun.

END

WATCH OUT FOR PAPERCUT乙™

Welcome to the fast and furry-ious, first BRINA THE CAT graphic novel, by Giorgio Salati, writer, and Christian Cornia, artist, from Papercutz, those fuzzy-wuzzy folks dedicated to publishing great graphic novels for all ages. I'm Jim Salicrup, the Editor-in-Chief and Chief Kitten Wrangler here to talk about cats. Seems that there are so many cats featured in our graphic novels, that it's often suggested that we change our name to Paper*catz*. Obviously we must love cats, with BRINA THE CAT being just the newest addition to our feline line-up. Here's a list of some of the other cats you'll find at Papercutz…

Azrael – This naughty kitty belongs to the Smurfs's arch foe, Gargamel. Azrael would love nothing better than to eat a Smurf! You can find Azrael in THE SMURFS graphic novels by Peyo (writer/artist).

Azrael

Cartoon – Is a pretty happy cat, and he lives with Chloe and her family. CHLOE, by Greg Tessier (writer) and Amandine (artist) is published by Charmz, an Papercutz imprint focused on young love. Even though Cartoon is a minor character in CHLOE, he's proven so popular that he'll soon have a graphic novel of his very own.

Cliff – Is the pet cat of the Loud family and is just one of the many occupants of THE LOUD HOUSE. There's Lincoln Loud, his ten sisters (Lori, Leni, Luna, Luan, Lynn, Lucy, Lisa, Lola, Lana, and Lily), his parents (Rita and Lynn Sr.), and the other pets, Charles (a dog), El Diablo (a snake), Hops (a frog), Walt (a bird), and Geo (a hamster). Cliff may not be the star of THE LOUD HOUSE, but the fact is that the Nickelodeon animated series is a big hit, as are the Papercutz graphic novels, so who's to say he's not a part of what's making THE LOUD HOUSE so successful?

Hubble – Is the snarky pet cat of the Monroe family, and the unofficial mascot of the GEEKY F@B 5. Hubble has watched sisters Lucy and Marina Monroe, start up the Geeky F@b 5 with their friends, Zara, A.J., and Sofia, and tackle all sorts of problems, including finding homes for pets when the local animal shelter suffers major damage from a tornado. Even Hubble has to admit that when girls stick together, anything is possible!

Pussycat – Before Peyo created THE SMURFS he wrote and drew the adventures of PUSSYCAT. Pussycat is a lovable, mischievous tuxedo cat who spends his time chasing after milk and snacks and framing other members of his family for his shenanigans. This cat isn't exactly the noble hunting type; he'd rather play a game of kickball with the resident mouse than chase after him. Warning, our hero Pussycat is a real cat. He does not speak (he just meows) and his main passions in life are eating, hunting mice, avoiding dogs and meowing at night. All of Pussycat's adventures were collected in one deluxe volume entitled, PUSSYCAT.

Pussycat

Scarlett – Scarlett, as revealed in SCARLETT "Star on the Run" by Jon Buller (author/artist) and Susan Schade (author/artist), is a small, harlequin-colored cat and a huge movie star. And what's more she talks! Unfortunately she's also abused by her producer, so she dreams of only one thing: escaping! When the occasion presents itself, she runs for her life.

Sushi – In CAT AND CAT by Christophe Cazenove (co-writer), Hervé Richez (co-writer), and Yrgane Ramon (artist), when Sushi is adopted by Cat (short for Catherine) and her dad, their quiet life of living alone is over. Between turning everything into either a personal scratching post or litter box, and the constant cat and mouse game of "love me/leave me alone," Sushi convinces Cat and her dad that they have a lot to learn about cats.

Sushi

Sybil – Is the cute cat owned by fourteen-year-old (soon to be fifteen) Amy Von Brandt. Amy's life is never dull, and you can find out all about her and Sybil in AMY'S DIARY by Véronique Grisseaux (writer) and Laëtitia Ayné(artist), based on the novels by India Desjardins, and published by Charmz.

We could go on and on, but we think you get the point! (We didn't even mention Geronimo Stilton's purr-sistant foes, the Pirate Cats, who in the GERONIMO STILTON graphic novels, are always trying to rewrite history to their advantage!) Instead, we'll just ask you to keep an eye out for the next BRINA THE CAT graphic novel, and to watch out for Papercutz!

Thanks,

Jim

STAY IN TOUCH!

EMAIL: salicrup@papercutz.com
WEB: papercutz.com
TWITTER: @papercutzgn
INSTAGRAM: @papercutzgn
FACEBOOK: PAPERCUTZGRAPHICNOVELS
FAN MAIL: Papercutz, 160 Broadway, Suite 700,
              East Wing, New York, NY 10038

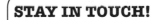

Brina's Tale

She's a big-city cat
With a window-pressed face,
Looking at the world
In a car that races,
Whizzing through the trees
As she heads to the hills,
Owners up front, she's
Calm and chill.

Margret and Sam
Once adopted that cat:
She lived with her mom
On a farm before that...
She can't remember much:
It's a flash and a blur
'Cause she was still tiny—
A little ball of fur!

The vacation's begun!
They love the fresh air:
A big book in the sun—
They haven't got a care!
But I spoke too soon:
I hear a loud meow!
It's Brina's ringing tune:
She wants out...NOW!

To let her out's scary.
Will she find her way back?
Brina's not wary—
She'll explore the outback!

She takes a few steps;
She finds some new friends...
The local Gang of Cats—
They're just around the bend:
A bunch of cranky strays
Who hunt and live like beasts:
"Be free, like us," they say,
"The forest's full of feasts!"

She really likes her humans—
Dearest Margret, friendly Sam—
But woods are fun to run in:
She heads out, on the lam!
She leaps, she hunts, she fishes,
Playing tricks with old cans!
There's water when she wishes
She steals cakes from hot pans!
Filled with jubilation
She's feline fancy-free;
She's joined the jungle nation:
"No more litter box for me!"

At home, the house is sad,
They miss their cat that fled.
They walk and put up ads
And hope she's getting fed.
They search throughout the woods,
Looking up and down.
Is Brina gone for good?
No one's seen her 'round town!

Living wild seems fun
With her furry new friends,
But there really is a ton
Of strife without an end.
With fights and selfish acts

Life's NOT a piece of cake;
The gang's a cage, in fact:
It feels just like a fake.

The gang's no good for her!
She leaves: she knows her mind...
They're spiteful! They tease her!
She'll leave them all behind.
She leaps into a tree
'Midst heavy winds and rain.
She yowls where none can see.
She meows her lonely pain.

Sam and Margret miss her;
They're thinking of their cat!
Brina's thoughts are all a-blur:
Her heart goes pitter-pat
'Bout the house she used to live in
Where a kitten once she was—
Owners in the kitchen
Filled with happy, warm buzz!
Now she knows a home
Is family, not a cage!
They miss her: Time to roam
Back where there's no rage.

The night is dark and wet—
Wild winds, the forest dim.
Is this the way? Did she forget?
She risks her life and limb!
A cat can use her eyes,
Her whiskers, and her nose.
Her heart knows! Now she flies
As homeward bound she goes!

Sam and Margret wake—
Their hope is not yet dead.
A meow? Their hearts still ache;
They hope she hasn't fled.
And so it comes to pass:
They open up their door;
The cat they missed, at last
Stands soaking: hugs galore!

She's wounded just a bit;
Her fur is caked with dirt.
Blankets, tears, delight:
They're glad she's not too hurt!

Now the time has come...
Back to city lights.
Farewell to country cats—
Her eyes are shining bright.
Her friends they only were
A day or two or three.
Next year again they'll see her
For vacation, here she'll be.
Goodbye to mountains high,
To fir and scented pine,
To sun and air so delicate,
To joy without a whine.

They all go back together,
Sam, Margret, and their cat.
They know what really counts in life
is love—and that's that.

Original text by Giorgio Salati
Translation and adaptation by Nanette McGuinness
Illustration by Cristina Giorgilli